Sven Nordqvist

Pettson Goes Camping

Opal

One day old man Pettson was up in his attic looking for a bag of fishing floats, which he thought were somewhere there. Findus, his cat, was helping him as usual. When Pettson lifted out a box Findus found a green sausage. A big, green sausage made out of canvas. He jumped up on it and balanced. When he walked forwards, it rolled backwards. When he walked backwards it rolled forwards. When he ran it rolled faster.

"Look, Pettson!" he called out.

Pettson looked up from his box.

"Yes, I can see. Be careful you don't roll down ... "

"Heeeelp!"

The sausage bounced down the steep stairs and the cat came sprawling after it.

Pettson hurried down.

"Findus! Are you all right? Did you hurt yourself?"

"Yes," the cat whined. "I think I broke my ears. Why do you have such dangerous sausages lying about the attic?" he scolded.

"That's a tent," Pettson said.

"What do you mean a tent? What's a tent?" Findus said.

"A house made out of canvas that you can sleep in if you are hiking in the fjelds for instance."

The cat stared at the old man as if he wasn't in his right mind.

"Are you supposed to sleep in it when you are out on a hike? Are you supposed to walk in your sleep, eh? With a sausage on your head, or what?"

"No, certainly not!" Pettson said patiently. "There's a rolled up tent inside the bag. I'll show you."

Pettson pulled out the tent and unfolded it. When he sensed the smell he remembered very clearly what it felt like to lie in a tent, although it was such a long time ago. How much fun they had had on that occasion when he was young. What if he should try it again? And he could take the opportunity to try out his new invention.

Findus found the tent opening and crawled inside.

"I want to sleep in here," he said. "Can't we go hiking in the fjelds? What are the fjelds?"

"They are high mountains in Lapland," Pettson said.

"We've a high mountain behind the workshop. We can go hiking there," Findus said.

"But that is not much of an adventure. We'll have done that in fifteen minutes," the old man thought.

"But Pettson, it doesn't have to be that much of an adventure. We can hike a while and then sleep in the tent."

"But I should like to try out my invention,"
Pettson said. "I suggest we take a long trip round
the lake and then afterwards camp half way and
fish, and we can sit there by the lake when the
sun goes down and grill perches over the fire."
"Yees, let's do that. Come on let's go," Findus
cried and ran out.
"Not so fast. I have to get my things ready first."
Tent, sleeping bag, rucksack, coffee pot, the
invention that was not quite ready ...
It took a long time to think of, and find, all the
things that had to be brought along.
The cat waited impatiently.

At last they set off, the cat first and then the old man. When they walked past some of the hens, Findus cried out:
"Goodbye hens! Now we're going camping and hiking in the fjelds and fishing in the lake and you can't come along."
"Why can't we come along? Pettson! We want to go camping in the lake too!" clucked the hens and ran after them.
"No, that's not possible," Pettson said. "You can't manage to walk that far. You'll just get lost in the forest and then the fox will come and eat you up. You're staying here!"
"We want to come along!" shrieked the hens.

Pettson started running, but the hens followed him.
Old Mrs. Andersson was standing in the beetfield and saw Pettson and
the hens.
"Don't be afraid of the hens, Pettson," she cried. "They're not as dangerous
as they look!"
Pettson stopped. This was just too silly. The hens must go back home again.

He went back and the hens followed him hesitantly. He went to the chicken-run and called to them:

"Come on now little hens, chick, chick! It's time to roost now. Come on, come on."

Findus ran around trying to drive them in. But of course that didn't work.

"He thinks we're stupid. It's the middle of the day! If you're going camping in the lake, Pettson, then we're coming with you. If you're staying here, then so are we."

The message was plain and that was the way it had to be. You can't decide over the heads of ten hens just like that.

"We'll have to go hiking another time instead, Findus," Pettson said. "At least you won't have to walk so far now."
Findus was disappointed, he jumped around insulting the hens. But when Pettson said that they could put up the tent in the garden instead, everyone was happy again. The cat helped and the hens watched and soon the tent was pitched.

Pettson rolled out the sleeping bag and Findus crawled into it. He looked pleased.
"This house is just right for me. I want to sleep here tonight."
"We want to sleep here tonight, too," said the hens.
"No! You can't," Findus cried out. "They can't, can they, Pettson?"
"It will sort itself out, no doubt," the old man said. "Come on Findus, I need your help with something."
When they were out of earshot of the hens Pettson whispered:
"Let them have their own way. They'll get tired soon. In the meantime we can go fishing. I'm going to try out my new invention."

Pettson had invented a fishing bow. Down by the lake he explained to Findus how it worked. The hook and the float were attached to an arrow. The arrow was attached to the fishing line. The rest of the line was wound onto a reel, which was attached to a bow. With it he could shoot the arrow with the hook far out into the water, much further than he could reach with the fishing rod. It worked quite superbly.

Pettson aimed for the clump of reeds further out. He was sure there were big pikes out there. For a long while nothing happened, other than that Findus caught one perch after another, where he was standing on a stone angling in the way people usually did.

Then Pettson took the smallest perch and put it on the hook and took a shot. The arrow had hardly gone down in the water when there was a splash. It was an enormous splash from an enormous fish.

"Look Findus," Pettson squealed. "Did you see? What a pike!"

It was as big as a seal; it struck again; Pettson held on to the bow for all he was worth, then the line snapped and disappeared with the pike down into the lake.

The old man and the cat stared in silence at the rings on the water until the lake was calm again.

"Oh my," Pettson whispered. "I've never seen such a big one before."

"Let's go home now," Findus said and ran a long way up on land. "Come on now Pettson! We have enough fish now."

On the way back Findus wanted to know everything about how big and dangerous pikes could be. But Pettson was very quiet and thoughtful and hardly answered. As long as the lake was in sight he kept turning round and looking back at the clump of reeds, but no more splashing was to be seen.

When they came back the hens, sure enough, had tired of being inside the tent. Only May Rose was still in the sleeping bag laying eggs.

Pettson lit a fire on the gravel path and made coffee over it. Then they grilled the perches over the embers and pretended they were in the fjelds. Pettson leaned back against the apple-tree and breathed a deep sigh.

"Oh! There's nothing like a grilled perch and a cup of coffee after a long day's hike in the fjelds. At least I don't think so."

"Don't you know?" Findus asked.

"No, I've never been in the fjelds. Never got round to it. We didn't have the time for things like that. And couldn't afford it either. But it would have been fun."

When it began to get dark Findus wanted to go to bed, though it wasn't very late. He wanted to sleep in the tent and didn't want to wait any longer. Pettson said: "Goodnight cat," went and shut in the hens and then went indoors to listen to the weather report. Findus lay alone in the tent. It was exciting to lie in a tent. There is a special light inside a tent and a special darkness, it was almost dark now. Sound was different too, he heard the soft rustle from the trees almost as clearly as outdoors, but yet in another way. Both more clearly and more subdued at the same time. Yes, he actually heard every little click and murmur more clearly. Since he could not see it he made twice the effort to try and figure out what kind of sound it was. No matter how much he looked, all he could see was the canvas and no matter how much he listened, he still wasn't sure what he heard, for instance he didn't know what a huge pike sounds like.

Suddenly it was much too exciting to be alone in a tent, he jumped up out of the sleeping bag, peeped through the tent opening, then ran as fast as he could into the kitchen, back to Pettson.

The old man was just going to bed when the cat came rushing in.

"What's this?" Pettson said. "Wasn't it fun to sleep in the tent?"

"Oh yes," Findus said. "It was fun for quite a while. But then it got so lonely. I think it would have been more fun if I hadn't been alone."

"Really, you don't say?" Pettson said. "I didn't think you were afraid of the dark; you who see so well in the dark."

"Yes, yes, you always say that. But I hear well too," Findus said. "And the thing is that when you're in a tent you only see the tent but you hear much more. So I thought that if you sat with me for a while I wouldn't hear so much, and then it would be much more fun to sleep in a tent."

"Yes, that's probably so," Pettson muttered.

"Yes, I suppose I could do that for a while, then we'll see how it goes."

They went out to the tent again. Now it was almost completely dark. Findus crawled into the sleeping bag and Pettson sat beside him. But it was a small tent and he wasn't sitting very comfortably, so after a while he lay down on the sleeping bag and put Findus inside his hat instead.

They were quiet for a little while, then Findus said:

"It was lucky anyway that you didn't land that pike. It would probably have eaten us up. I don't think I want to come along next time you're going fishing."

"You don't have to be afraid of that. As I've never seen anything as big before, we'll probably never see it again," Pettson said. "Go to sleep now."

And then he fell asleep, Pettson that is.

And before Findus had noticed that he was alone again he fell asleep too.

Findus woke up early next morning, before it had become quite light. He felt cold and was thirsty. He ran into the house and drank some milk. Then he went into Pettson's bedroom and took the opportunity to jump around on his bed for a while, because the old man did not like this when he saw it, but he couldn't see it now. Then he thought that to crawl under the quilt was so soft and warm, so he stayed there for a while. Just a little while, before he would go out to the tent again. Besides what was he going to do there. He could just as well stay here and enjoy being comfortable.

Findus woke up to the sound of the biggest pike in the world knocking on the door. Wide awake he jumped out of bed and listened. The kitchen door opened and the pike stepped in and called out: "Hello! Pettson! Are you awake?" It was Gustavsson, the neighbour. Findus kept quiet. He did not like Gustavsson. He jumped out of the window and ran inside the tent and woke Pettson up.

Before the old man was quite awake Gustavsson came and peered into the tent.

"Hello there, Pettson. It's eight o'clock. Time to get up."

Pettson grunted and, with difficulty, started crawling out of the tent.

"So, you're out camping," Gustavsson said. "Are you on holiday?"

Pettson was ashamed, since his neighbour had caught him sleeping in a tent in his own garden. People don't usually do that kind of thing.

"No, not exactly," he mumbled. He didn't know what he should say. "It's not me ... it's Findus."

"Really, it's Findus, is it," Gustavsson said and stroked his chin. "But it looks like you. At least it's the same hat."

Gustavsson grinned in such a way that Pettson realised that before the day was over, the whole neighbourhood would know that silly Pettson was on a camping holiday in his own garden.

At that point Pettson got angry.

"I realise that you need something new to tell the neighbours," he said. "In that case I'll tell you all about it. We've been out hiking in the fjelds for a couple of days, Findus and me. At Sulitelma we were pursued by a flock of white wolves, so we got lost. We ended up in the Torne Marsh and there we did some fishing. I landed the great lake monster with my bow, but I threw it back in. Findus caught a few salmon. Afterwards we went home and ate them and then I became so full up that I fell asleep. And now when I woke up I was lying in the tent. It must have been Findus who pitched the tent over me. While I was asleep. Is that right, Findus?" The cat nodded.

"I told you so. That's how it happened," Pettson said. "I hope you don't mind me taking a nap in my own garden."

"No, no, not at all." Gustavsson said. He looked quite dumbfounded. He didn't know what to believe.

"I just wanted to borrow a pipe wrench," he said.

They went to the workshop. Gustavsson got his pipe wrench and made his way home, still pensive.

"You can borrow the tent too," Pettson called out after him. "If you want to go on holiday with your family. Take the cows too, they can need to get out a bit!"

Gustavsson did not reply.

"Why did you tell him all that made-up story?" Findus said.

"Well, if he is going to go round gossiping anyway, he might as well have a proper story to tell. Camping in the garden isn't much to talk about."

"Hey, Pettson," Findus said, "we forgot to go hiking in the fjelds."

"Yes, that's right, we'll have to do that now instead then. We can go up on the hill behind the workshop and have breakfast."

"Yees, let's do that! Come on Pettson, let's go!"

© Sven Nordqvist 1992
Bokförlaget Opal AB
Translation: Martin Peterson
Printed in Belgium 2003
ISBN: 91-7299-056-2